No.1 HITS
Playalong *for* Flute

WISE PUBLICATIONS
London/New York/Paris/Sydney/Copenhagen/Madrid

Exclusive Distributors:
Music Sales Limited
8/9 Frith Street, London W1V 5TZ, England.
Music Sales Pty Limited
120 Rothschild Avenue, Rosebery, NSW 2018, Australia.

Order No. AM955614
ISBN 0-7119-7366-0
This book © Copyright 1999 by Wise Publications.

Book design by Michael Bell Design.
Music arranged by Paul Honey.
Music processed by Enigma Music Production Services.
Cover photography by George Taylor.
Printed in the United Kingdom by Page Bros., Norwich, Norfolk.

CD produced by Paul Honey.
Instrumental solos by John Whelan.
Engineered by Kester Sims.

Your Guarantee of Quality:
As publishers, we strive to produce every book to
the highest commercial standards.
The music has been freshly engraved and the book has been
carefully designed to minimise awkward page turns and
to make playing from it a real pleasure.
Particular care has been given to specifying acid-free, neutral-sized
paper made from pulps which have not been elemental chlorine bleached.
This pulp is from farmed sustainable forests and was
produced with special regard for the environment.
Throughout, the printing and binding have been planned to
ensure a sturdy, attractive publication which should give years of enjoyment.
If your copy fails to meet our high standards,
please inform us and we will gladly replace it.

Music Sales' complete catalogue describes thousands of
titles and is available in full colour sections by subject,
direct from Music Sales Limited.
Please state your areas of interest and send a
cheque/postal order for £1.50 for postage to:
Music Sales Limited, Newmarket Road, Bury St. Edmunds, Suffolk IP33 3YB.

www.guestspot.com

Fingering Guide

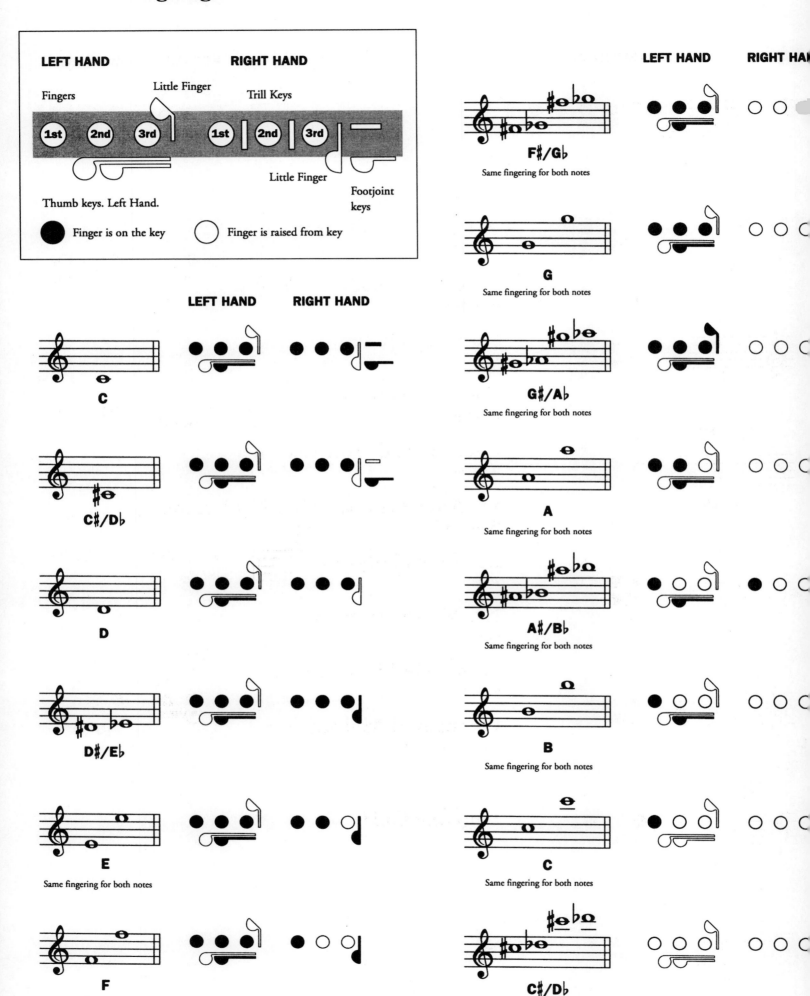

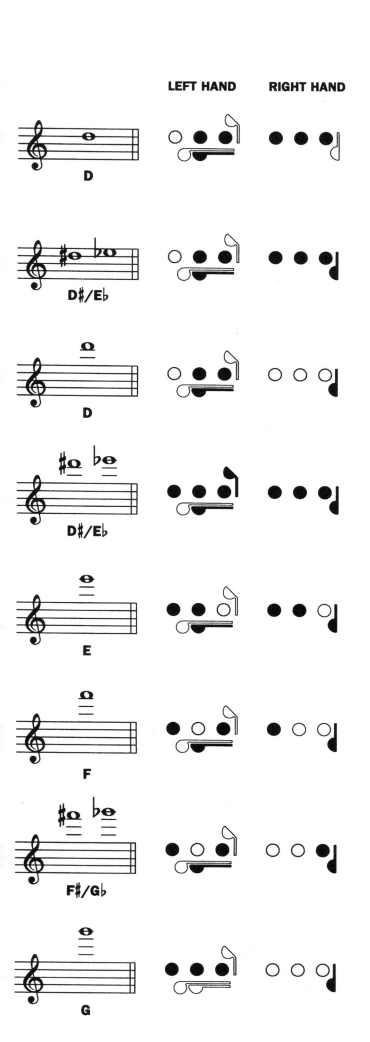
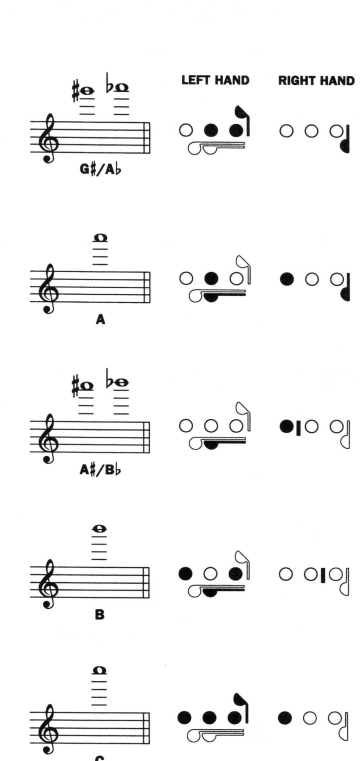

A Whiter Shade Of Pale

Words & Music by Keith Reid & Gary Brooker

A Hard Day's Night

Words & Music by John Lennon & Paul McCartney

Slower

Dancing Queen

Words & Music by Benny Andersson, Stig Anderson & Bjorn Ulvaeus

Moderate rock

12

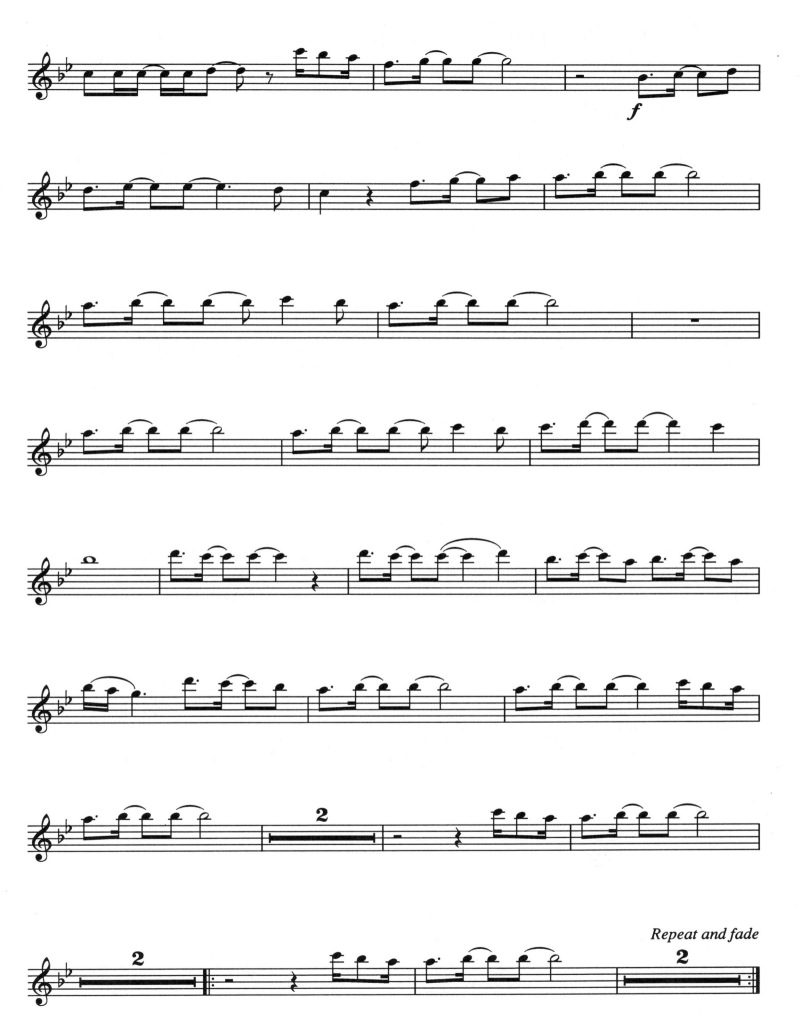

Repeat and fade

Every Breath You Take

Words & Music by Sting

Moderately

He Ain't Heavy... He's My Brother

Words by Bob Russell
Music by Bobby Scott

Rather slow

Eternal Flame

Words & Music by Billy Steinberg, Tom Kelly & Susanna Hoffs

Moderately

dim.

22

Mull Of Kintyre

Words & Music by McCartney & Laine

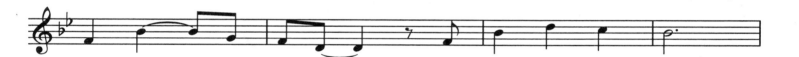

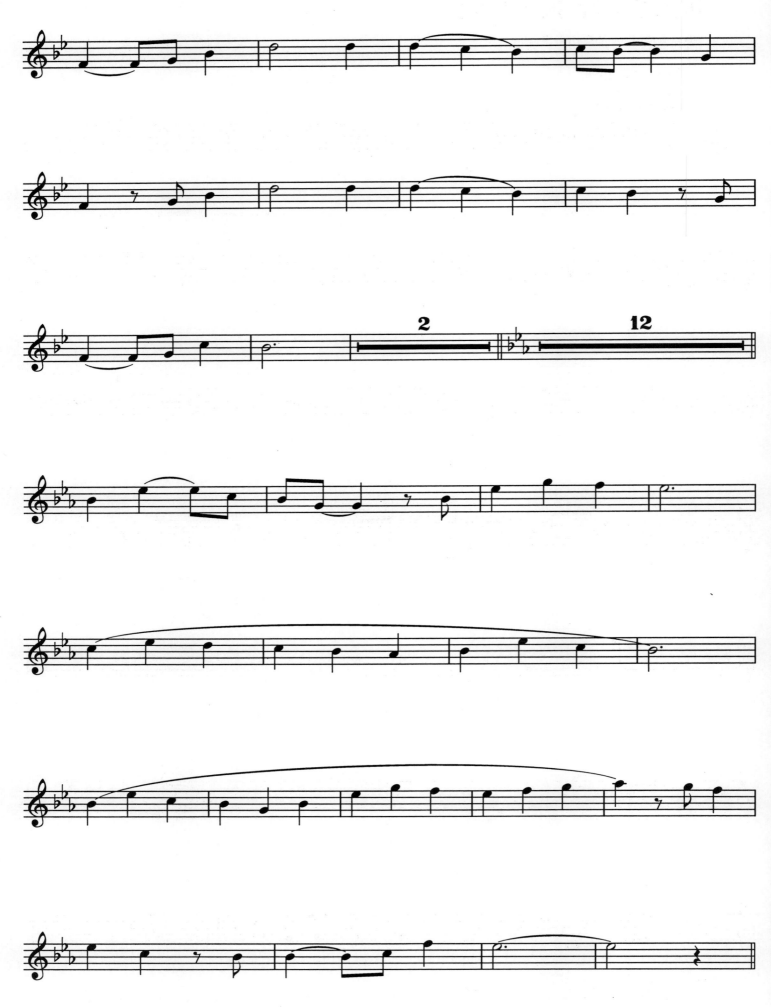

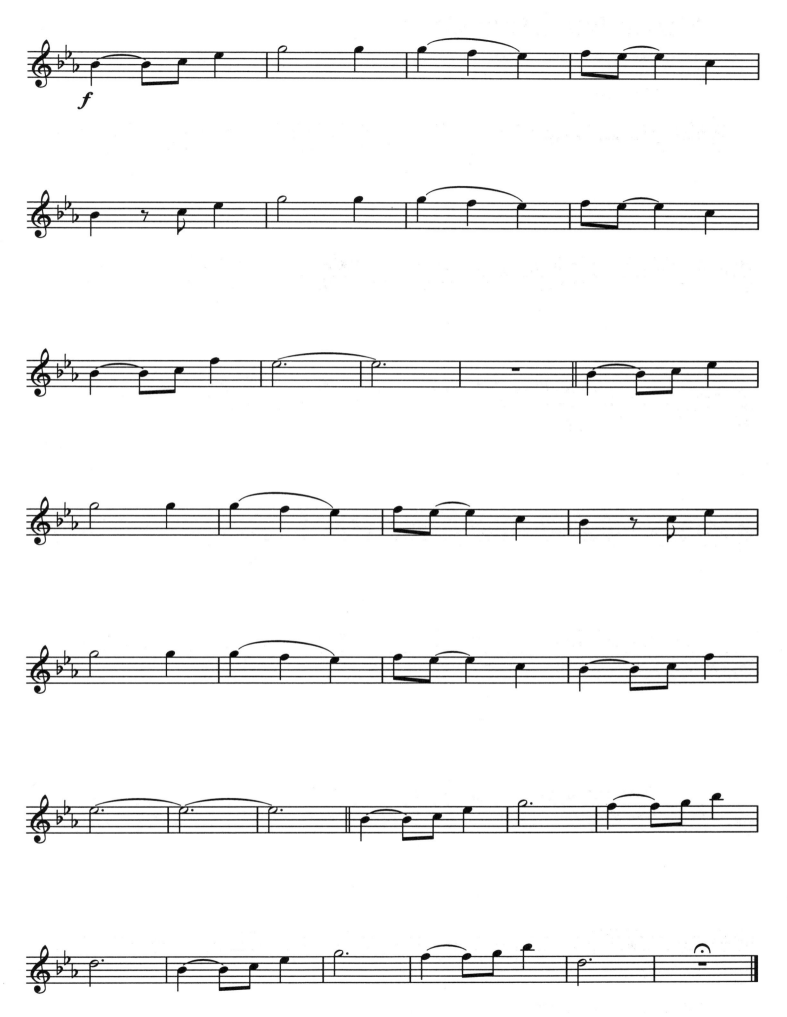

Show Me Heaven

Words & Music by Maria McKee, Jay Rifkin & Eric Rackim

Unchained Melody

Words by Hy Zaret
Music by Alex North

molto rall.

No Matter What

Music by Andrew Lloyd Webber
Lyrics by Jim Steinman